Starring in

Gorilla My Dreams

Starring in
Gorilla My Dreams

By **Ellen Conford**
Illustrated by **Renee W. Andriani**

SCHOLASTIC INC.
New York Toronto London Auckland Sydney
Mexico City New Delhi Hong Kong

ISBN 0-439-27136-3

Text copyright © 1999 by Ellen Conford.
Illustrations copyright © 1999 by Renee W. Andriani. All rights reserved.
Published by Scholastic Inc., 555 Broadway, New York, NY 10012, by
arrangement with Simon & Schuster Books for Young Readers,
an imprint of Simon & Schuster Children's Publishing Division.
SCHOLASTIC and associated logos are trademarks and/or registered
trademarks of Scholastic Inc.

12 11 10 9 8 7 6 5 4 3 2 1   2 3 4 5/0

Printed in the U.S.A.   40

First Scholastic printing, January 2001

Book design by Lucille Chomowicz
The text for this book is in Berkeley Book.

The black-and-white illustrations for this book
were done with crowquill pen and ink.
The cover art is pen-and-ink colored with watercolor and artists' dyes.
Cover design by Anahid Hamparian

For Celeste and Bill Watman
—E. C.

For Ellen, Joseph, and Maggie
—R. W . A.

Annabel, the Actress

Annabel was an actress.

Every week she put an ad in the town newspaper. The paper printed free ads for kids who wanted jobs.

Annabel's ad read:

ANNABEL THE ACTRESS.
NO PART TOO BIG OR TOO SMALL.

Annabel wanted to be a movie star someday. Or at least a soap opera star.

When she watched TV, she studied how the actors acted.

When she went to the movies, she

imagined how she would play the starring roles.

Sometimes she thought, *I could do that.* Sometimes she thought, *I could do* better *than that.*

She read all the books she could find in the library about acting.

And she practiced all the time.

Today she was acting angry.

She stood in front of a mirror. She made her face look snarly. She messed up her hair. She held her hands out like claws.

"I hate you!" she shouted at the mirror. "Hate you, hate you, hate you!"

That's pretty good anger, she thought.

But it's not great *anger.*

She tried to think of things that made her angry: Homework on a weekend. Losing all her money in Monopoly. Lowell Boxer making fun of her.

Lowell Boxer was her lifelong enemy.

She pretended Lowell Boxer was in the mirror.

"Grr! You get out of here, Lowell! *Or else!*"

Now that's great anger, Annabel thought. The important thing about acting was feeling the part. And she almost always felt angry at Lowell Boxer.

The phone rang.

"Hello!" shouted Annabel. "What do you want?"

"My, you sound angry," the caller said.

"Thank you," said Annabel. "I'm not really angry. I was just practicing acting angry."

"Then you must be Annabel," the caller said. "I saw your ad in the newspaper."

"I am Annabel," Annabel said. "Do you need an actress?"

"I need a gorilla."

"Then why did you call an actress?" Annabel asked.

"What I mean is, I need someone to play the part of a gorilla," the caller said.

"For a movie?" Annabel asked hopefully. "Or a TV show?"

"For my little brother's birthday party."

"Oh," said Annabel. Just a kid's party. She wouldn't have a very big audience. And there probably wouldn't be any show business people there.

But a job was a job.

"I want a gorilla to carry in the cake and sing 'Happy Birthday,'" the caller said.

"I can sing," Annabel said. "And dance, too. But maybe not while I'm carrying a cake."

"How much would you charge?" the caller asked. "You would only have to be here for about half an hour."

Annabel thought about it. "Ten dollars," she said.

"That seems fair," said the caller. "But you sound like a kid."

"I am a kid," said Annabel. "Do you think a grown-up would work that cheap?"

"It's just that Dennis likes big gorillas. You might be too short."

"I am an actress," Annabel said. "I will act tall."

"Well, okay. The price is right, anyhow. My

name is Daisy Fry. Our address is 462 Washington Street."

Annabel wrote it down. "Is your brother Dennis Fry?" she asked. "The one who got stuck on his roof?"

"That's Dennis." Daisy sighed. "We had quite a crowd here that day."

"I know," said Annabel. "I saw the firemen get him down."

"You must live pretty near us," Daisy said.

"Yes," said Annabel, "so I will not need a limo."

"You have a limo?" Daisy sounded impressed.

"No," said Annabel. "That's why I'm glad I won't need one."

"Be here at two o'clock Saturday," Daisy said. "And come in the back door. I don't want Dennis to see you. By the way—you do have a gorilla costume, don't you?"

"Of course," said Annabel. "Doesn't everyone?"

"Okay," said Daisy. "See you Saturday, then."

"Wait!" Annabel said. "How old is Dennis?"

"He'll be five on Saturday."

"Are you sure you want a gorilla?" asked Annabel. "Gorillas can be pretty scary."

"Dennis loves gorillas," Daisy said. "*King Kong* is his favorite movie."

"All right," said Annabel. "You're the director. I just hope I don't scare him."

"You don't sound very scary," Daisy said.

"That's because I haven't gotten into the

part yet," Annabel told her. "By Saturday I'll be terrifying."

She hung up the phone.

She had a part!

It was only a children's birthday party. But all great actors have to start somewhere. And she would be paid ten dollars. For only half an hour of acting!

Now all she had to do was find a gorilla costume.

Maggie, the Costume Designer

In the basement was a box of old clothes. Annabel started to look through it.

She found torn pajamas, shrunken underwear, and mittens with holes in the thumbs.

She tossed aside flannel nightgowns and faded jeans and unmatched socks.

She didn't find anything that looked like a gorilla costume.

At the bottom of the box, Annabel felt something fuzzy. She pulled out a raincoat. The lining was dark brown. It felt like fur.

Annabel closed her eyes. She pictured a gorilla. Dark. Fuzzy. Hairy.

"Yes!"

She unzipped the lining from the raincoat and ran upstairs to the living room.

She pulled the lining over her shoulders.

Now at least, she told herself, *I look a little like a gorilla. Now I can get into my part.*

She thought about gorillas. How did they act? How did they walk? What did they sound like?

She bent her knees. She let her arms hang down. She shuffled across the living room, dragging her hands along the floor.

She scratched under her arms. She pounded her chest with her fists. She jumped onto a chair and made grunting noises.

Her mother came into the room.

Annabel jumped off the chair. She bounced toward her mother, squealing and scratching herself.

"What are you doing?" her mother asked. "You look like a monkey."

"Good," said Annabel. "I'm trying to look

like a gorilla. I'll just work my way up."

Annabel told her about the party. "I'd rather be a ballerina, though. Or a cat. Or a princess."

Her mother nodded. "You'd like to wear a pretty costume."

"No," said Annabel, "I'd like to wear a costume I've got."

The doorbell rang. Annabel's mother went to answer it.

"Maggie!" Annabel cried. "Just the person I wanted to see!"

"You see me all the time." Maggie came into the living room.

She was dressed in a leather vest and pin-striped pants. She had on a black hat with a wide brim. A long string of pearls hung down to her belt.

Maggie was a very snappy dresser.

"But I really needed to see you today," Annabel said.

She told her about her gorilla job.

"The only thing is, I don't have a

costume." Annabel showed Maggie the
raincoat lining. "I got this out of the junky
clothes box in my basement.

"Can I have it for my costume?" she
asked her mother.

"Sure," she said. "You can use anything
you find in that box."

Annabel's mother left the girls alone.

"Do you think you can help me make a
gorilla costume?" Annabel asked Maggie.
"Out of this?"

Maggie loved clothes. She was always
drawing pictures of outfits she would like to
wear.

But Annabel didn't think she'd ever designed a gorilla costume.

Maggie looked at the lining. She held it up against Annabel.

"Hmm," she said. "This might be tricky. I'm not sure you have enough for a whole gorilla."

"It's got to be enough," said Annabel. "There isn't any more."

"I'll do my best," said Maggie. "But you'll have to be a short-sleeved gorilla."

She told Annabel to get a pair of scissors and some pins. Then she spread the raincoat lining on the floor.

"Lie down on it," she said. "And hold out your arms. Like you're making snow angels."

Annabel lay down on the lining. Maggie began to cut the material around her.

"Ooch," Maggie grunted.

"What's the matter?"

"This is really thick," said Maggie. "It's hard to get the scissors through it."

The cutting went very slowly. Maggie said "ooch" a lot. But finally it was done.

Annabel stood up. Maggie pinned the pieces of lining around her. She stood back and looked at Annabel. She tilted her head to one side. She tapped her finger against her chin.

"Yes," she said at last. "I think it will work."

"I knew you could do it!" Annabel hugged her. "When I'm a star, you will design all my costumes."

Maggie rubbed her sore hand. "Not if they're made of fur," she said.

"Now all I need is a gorilla face," Annabel said. She picked up the leftover pieces of fur. There were only a few little strips and squares left.

"Do you think we could make something with these?"

Maggie looked at the scraps of fur. "Maybe we could make some eyebrows and a mustache," she said. "But I don't think we can make a whole face."

"What I need," said Annabel, "is a makeup artist. When I am a famous actress, I will have my own personal makeup artist. Then I won't have these problems."

"When you're a famous actress," Maggie said, "you probably won't have to play a gorilla."

"I hope not," Annabel said. "But I've got to be one by Saturday. I'll just have to do my own makeup."

"How?" asked Maggie.

Annabel sighed deeply. "I have no idea."

After Maggie left, Annabel put the scraps of fur in a circle on the floor. She tried to fit them together like a jigsaw puzzle.

Maybe, she thought, *just maybe . . .*

She gathered them up and took them to her room. She got a glue stick from her desk drawer. She found a black eyeliner pencil she'd once used to draw whiskers for her cat costume.

She read the writing on the glue stick.

It didn't say, POISON! or, DO NOT PUT ON FACE! It didn't say, THIS WILL NEVER COME OFF!

So Annabel turned over the stick and started dabbing glue on her cheeks.

She pressed the pieces of lining against the gluey spots on her face.

Some of them stuck. Some of them fell off.

She tried to make a fierce gorilla face. All of the pieces fell off.

She pressed them back on again. She tried not to move her mouth. She tried not to move her eyebrows.

She rubbed eyeliner all over her nose.

The phone rang. She went into her parents' room to answer it.

"Guess what?" Maggie yelled, without even saying "Hello."

"What?"

"Oliver has a gorilla mask!"

Oliver was Maggie's older brother.

"He said you could borrow it," Maggie added.

"Why didn't you tell me?" A piece of fur fell off Annabel's chin.

"I forgot he had it," Maggie said. "He only wore it twice. Once on Halloween, and once when he ran for class president."

"That's great!" Annabel said.

"But you have to take really good care of it," Maggie said. "He may run for class president again."

"I'll guard it with my life," Annabel promised. "Is it a scary mask?"

"It's gross," Maggie said.

"Excellent," said Annabel.

Lowell, the Bad Guy

Annabel rehearsed her gorilla part all week.

Her mother asked her to stop climbing up the bookcase.

Her father asked her to stop picking at his ears.

"I'm grooming you," Annabel told him. "I'm taking the fleas out of your fur."

"I don't have any fleas in my fur," her father said. "I don't have *fur*."

"You would if you were a gorilla."

Her teacher, Mr. Doyle, asked her why she was walking all stooped over. "Did you hurt your back?"

"Not yet," said Annabel. "But I will if I keep walking this way."

Saturday morning, Maggie brought the finished gorilla costume over.

"I can't wait to see it on you," she told Annabel.

Annabel held up the costume. "Why are all these things sticking out of it?"

"The lining was so thick I couldn't push a needle through," Maggie said. "So I used safety pins."

Annabel had never seen a gorilla with safety pins. But she didn't want to hurt Maggie's feelings. She started to put on the costume.

"Not that way," Maggie said. "The pins go on the inside, so they won't show."

"Ooh," said Annabel. "That will look much better."

Maggie helped her put on the costume. She pinned it closed in the back. "Perfect!" she said.

Annabel turned and looked in the mirror.

The costume was not exactly perfect. The arms only came down to her elbows. The legs were tight and bunched up on the sides.

"Put on the mask," Maggie said.

Annabel pulled the mask over her head. The eye holes came down below her cheeks. "I can't see."

"You'd better carry it to the party," Maggie

said. "Especially if you have to cross any streets."

"But how am I going to see what I'm doing at the party?"

Maggie put her hands on her hips. "I made the costume," she said. "I got you a mask. I don't think you should be so picky."

"You're right," Annabel said. "You've been a huge help. And I still want you to be my costume designer when I'm famous."

"But no fur," Maggie reminded her.

"No fur," Annabel agreed. She gazed at herself in the mirror. Except for the mask, she didn't look very much like a gorilla.

This, she thought, *is going to be one tough acting job.*

At one thirty, Annabel started for the Frys' house. It was only a few blocks away, but she needed time to get into her character.

She bent her knees. She dragged her fingers along the sidewalk. She made snorting sounds. "Unnff! Unnff!"

Ahead of her, Mr. Schultz and his dog, Trixie, turned to stare. Mr. Schultz crossed to the other side of the street.

Annabel stood up and pounded her fists against her chest. Trixie yapped wildly.

Mr. Schultz scooped his dog up in his arms. He hurried off toward his house.

By the time Annabel reached Washington Street she was feeling her part. She might be a short-sleeved gorilla, but she was fierce and powerful.

And then, on the opposite corner, she saw Lowell Boxer.

"Oh, no!" She groaned. "My lifelong enemy!"

If he saw her, he'd chase her. Or tease her. Or mess up her costume.

He always chased her. And teased her.

Maggie said it was because he secretly liked her. Annabel thought it was because he was just a bad guy.

But he wouldn't dare mess with King Kong, Annabel told herself. Quickly she put the gorilla mask over her head.

"I am Kong the Mighty," she told herself. "I am huge. I am scary. I am Lowell Boxer's worst nightmare."

"I see you, Annabel!" Lowell charged across the street. "You can't fool me. That mask looks just like your face."

Annabel tried to stay in her part. "I am Kong the Mighty!" she roared.

"You are Annabel the Teeny Weeny!" Lowell grabbed at the mask. He yanked it right off Annabel's head.

"You give that back!" she yelled.

Lowell started to run. Annabel ran after him.

"Give me my mask!"

Lowell raced around the corner of Washington Street. Annabel chased after him.

Suddenly she felt something scratching her leg. "Ouch!"

Something sharp jabbed her shoulder. "OUCH!"

The safety pins. They were popping open.

Annabel reached under her costume. She felt around for the pins.

"Ow! Ow! Ow! Lowell Boxer, you come back—OW!"

But Lowell was nowhere to be seen.

This was terrible.

Her mask was gone. Her costume was stabbing her. She didn't feel a bit like Kong the Mighty.

She felt like Annabel the Teeny Weeny.

Carefully she stepped out of her costume. She turned it inside out. She pulled it back

on. Now the safety pins were on the outside,
so they couldn't stab her.

I can still be a gorilla, Annabel thought. *I
practiced being a gorilla all week. I can grunt
and scratch and walk like a gorilla. I am an
actress.*

She looked down at herself. She looked
like a girl in a torn raincoat lining.

No matter how good an actress she was,
no one would believe she was King Kong.
Not even a five-year-old.

There was no time to get the mask back.

But she had to be fuzzy. Even if it hurt.

Lots of actors suffered for their art.

She pulled the costume off again. She closed all the safety pins she could reach. She turned the furry side out. She put it back on.

She hoped the pins wouldn't open again. But if they did, she would just have to suffer. She was an actress.

And the show must go on.

ACT FOUR:

Gorilla My Dreams

Annabel knocked on the back door of the Frys' house.

A teenage girl opened the door.

"Who are you?" she asked.

"I am Annabel," Annabel said. "Your gorilla."

Daisy Fry stared at her. "You call that a gorilla costume?"

"It is a gorilla costume," Annabel said. "Mostly. A bad guy stole some of it."

"You don't look anything like King Kong," Daisy said. "Dennis is going to be very disappointed."

Annabel felt a safety pin pop open. "Ouch!"

"What's the matter?" Daisy asked.

"I'm suffering for my art," Annabel said. "I might even bleed a little."

"I don't want you to suffer," Daisy said. "I just wanted King Kong."

There was a big birthday cake on the kitchen table. Next to it were some party hats. One was a gold cardboard crown.

Suddenly, Annabel knew how to play her part.

"If I can use that crown," she said, "everything will be fine."

Daisy sighed. "I don't see how a crown

will make you into King Kong," she said.
"But it's too late to get another gorilla."

She lit the candles on the cake. Annabel
put on the crown.

"When we start singing 'Happy Birthday,'"
Daisy said, "you come in with the cake."

Annabel nodded.

Daisy stopped at the kitchen door. She
turned back to look at Annabel. She shook
her head. Then she opened the door and
went into the next room.

Annabel picked up the cake platter. She
waited for her cue.

"Happy birthday to you..."

She pushed the door open with her foot.

"Happy birthday to you!" she sang.
"Happy birthday dear Dennis—"

The five little boys in the room screamed.

They rushed toward her. They jumped for the cake. They pulled at her costume. They all started shouting at once.

"Who are you? You're fuzzy! You look stupid! Give us some cake!"

Annabel put the cake down on the dining room table. She stood up tall. She tried to feel gorilla strength. She tried to feel gorilla power.

"I am Kong the Mighty!" She pounded her chest.

"No you're not!" The boy wearing the biggest hat jumped on a chair. "Kong is a hundred feet tall!"

"I am Queen Kong!" Annabel roared. "Queen of the jungle. And I'm hungry! Hungry for a birthday boy!"

She pounced at Dennis. He jumped off the chair, giggling. He ran behind his sister.

"GAHHRR!" Annabel pounded her chest. "Ow."

Dennis peered at her from behind Daisy. "What's the matter?"

Annabel held out her arm. She tried to keep the safety pin away from her skin.

"Um—an evil hunter shot me," she said. "With a poison dart."

"Wow!" The boys yelled. "Is the dart still in you? Let's see it! Can we pull it out? Are you going to die?"

"No one can destroy the mighty Queen Kong!" Annabel raised her fist in the air. "Ow."

"Let's see the dart! Let's see the dart!"

The boys threw themselves at Annabel. They pulled at her fur. They poked under her arms.

"Ouch! Cut it out!" Annabel cried. "You guys are worse than the evil hunter!"

This was not going well at all. Her audience was out of control. She had to do something to entertain them before they flattened her. She thought fast. A song? A dance? A dancing gorilla? Yes!

She caught Dennis by the shoulders.

"You can help me get rid of the poison," she said.

"How?" asked Dennis.

"By dancing," she said. "And cake. Dancing will make the poison get out of my body fast. And cake will make me strong again."

She bent her knees. She let her arms hang
down. She twisted her head to one side. She
began to tap-dance. The way she thought a
gorilla might tap-dance.

"Gorilla my dreams," she sang, "I love
you." She made her voice low and growly.
"Gorilla my dreams, you're hairy."

The boys all stared at her.

"What's wrong with you people?" she
roared. "Haven't you ever seen a gorilla tap-
dance before?"

She grabbed Dennis's hand. "Come on.

You have to dance with me."

Dennis started moving beside her, trying to tap like Annabel.

"Everybody!" Annabel ordered. "Everybody dance with Queen Kong!"

Dennis stopped trying to tap-dance. He began to stamp his feet and jump in circles. The other boys soon joined in.

They hopped around Annabel, singing "Gorilla my dreams" with her. They waved their arms in the air. They yelled, "Get the

poison out! Get the poison out!"

A few of the boys accidentally stomped on her feet.

Finally Annabel couldn't dance another step.

"The poison is gone now," she panted. "You saved me."

"Yay!" the boys cheered.

"Now we need cake."

"Yay!" the boys cheered. They all ran to watch Dennis and Daisy cut the cake.

Dennis handed the first piece of cake to Annabel. She took a plastic fork and nibbled a small bite.

"That's not how gorillas eat!" Dennis said. "Gorillas smush the food right into their mouth!"

Annabel looked at Dennis. She looked at the other party guests. She thought about how much she had suffered for her art. She had danced till she thought she would faint. The boys had poked at her till she felt like a pincushion. The safety pin under her arm was still sticking her.

She thought about Lowell Boxer and how he'd ruined her costume and stolen Oliver's mask.

She decided she had suffered enough.

"You have to smush!" Dennis insisted. "You have to smush your cake."

Annabel gave him a long, hard stare. "I am a queen," she said firmly. "Queens do not smush."

After the cake, Annabel bowed to the boys. "Thank you," she said. "You were a wonderful audience."

"Don't go!" they yelled. "Dance some more!"

"I can't," Annabel said. "The evil hunter is still out there. I must find him."

In the kitchen, Daisy gave her a ten-dollar bill.

"You were great," she said. "Even if you didn't look like a gorilla."

"The costume doesn't make the gorilla," Annabel said. "The actor makes the gorilla."

Annabel was proud as she left the Frys' house. She had not disappointed her audience. She had given a good performance.

And she had earned ten dollars.

But the Bad Guy still had Oliver's mask.

And if she didn't get it back, Oliver would be mad at her. Maggie would be mad at her.

She had to find a way to make Lowell give her back the mask.

Or else there wouldn't be a happy ending.

ACT FIVE:

The Happy Ending

Annabel heard a loud yell from Lowell Boxer's yard.

"Ay-eee—iii—ee-yii!"

She went around back. Lowell was on his jungle gym. He was hanging from the bars by one arm, wearing Oliver's gorilla mask.

Annabel was so angry she wanted to jump on the bars and grab the mask off Lowell's face.

But Lowell was bigger than she was. She couldn't fight him. He could run faster. She couldn't chase him.

She had to beat him with her brains. And her acting.

But how? Lowell was so mean that

Annabel didn't know what kind of acting
would convince him to give back the mask.

She could cry. She was good at acting sad.
But Lowell liked to make people cry. That
wouldn't work.

She could act angry. She had practiced
anger a lot. But Lowell wasn't afraid of her.
He wouldn't care if she was angry at him.

I have to scare him, Annabel thought. *I have
to scare him into giving me back the mask.* But
what would scare Lowell Boxer?

Suddenly Annabel remembered a movie
she had seen last Saturday. It was called *Silent*

Germ, Deadly Germ. It was about a killer virus that nearly wiped out the whole world.

It was very scary.

Annabel remembered how she felt while she was watching the movie.

I am frightened, she said to herself. *I am terrified. The virus has got me and I am very, very sick.*

She took a deep breath, opened her eyes wide, and ran into Lowell's yard.

"Oh, no!" she screamed. She staggered around the yard a little, moaning. "It's too late! Too late!"

"What's the matter with you?" Lowell asked.

"Stopplemayer's Virus," Annabel wailed. "And now you've got it too!"

"Are you crazy?" Lowell pulled the mask up so he could see her better.

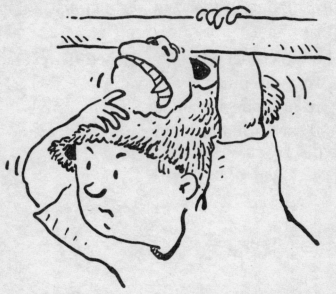

"Not yet," Annabel said. She held her hand to her heart. She made her lip tremble. "You get crazy later. First you turn green. And your hair falls out."

Lowell climbed down from the jungle

gym. "What are you talking about?"

Annabel looked at him sadly. "I know we're not friends," she said. "But I never wanted to make you sick."

"I'm not sick," Lowell said.

"You will be." Annabel sat down on the grass. She put her head in her hands. "Oh, if only you hadn't put on that mask."

"How could I get sick from a mask?" Lowell asked.

Annabel held her hands out toward Lowell. "Are they green yet?" she asked. "I'm afraid to look."

He walked slowly toward her. "I don't see any green." He looked at his own hands. "I'm not green either."

Annabel made a little choking sound. She coughed a few times. "Maybe we can share a room in the hospital," she said.

"I don't need to go to the hospital!" Lowell yelled.

"You will soon," Annabel said. "Everyone who gets Stopplemayer's Virus has to go to the hospital." She sighed deeply. "Even though there's no cure."

"I haven't got Stop— Stop— whatever that is!" Lowell cried.

"Oh, you'll get it," Annabel said. "The mask was on my face. The germs were on the mask. And you put on the mask." She shook her head hopelessly. "You are doomed."

Lowell stared at her, his eyes wide with horror. For a moment Annabel thought he really did look a little green.

Then he screamed. "Mom! Mommy!"

He tossed the mask at Annabel and raced across the yard. He ran into the house, still screaming for his mother.

Annabel stood up and brushed some
loose grass off her gorilla costume. She
picked up the mask.

"Stopplemayer's Virus." She giggled.
"Lowell should really watch more movies."

She walked out of the Boxers' yard with

Oliver's mask tucked safely under her arm.

Whistling "There's No Business Like Show Business," she turned the corner and headed for home.

Annabel just loved happy endings.